helios and his moon

nicholas mcdaniel

3

table of contents

acknowledgments

this book was a challenge to write. not
because of any creative difficulties, but
simply because i felt this topic was lost from
me. i cannot stress how much i'd like to
thank my friends and family for constant
support. all the times i've heard "there's no
way you're writing a book" just makes me
want to prove them wrong even more. i'd
also like to thank my partner, who gave me
the courage and inspiration to follow this
dream. many poems are based on her, (the
positive ones, of course) so really, it
wouldn't have been possible without her. i
love each and every one of you who
supported me, you know who you are. and,
most importantly, i love each and every one
of you who is reading this book. this is for
you.

her helios

the following poems are of everything positive within a relationship. it may be about attraction, lust, love, and the likes. some poems stretch the same idea amongst multiple pages, while others are only a few words. regardless, the love one feels for another is the strength that holds souls together. the strength that pulls helios towards his moon.

god may list you as
his most beautiful creation
bringing him happiness as
he watches you light up the world

if god were to put his faith within you
it would be for a good reason
as he watches you plant the seeds of heaven
wherever
you are.

i am on my knees

i am praying to a goddess who doesn't know
me

a goddess who cries at night
contemplating her mortality

or lack thereof

i am praying to a goddess who doesn't know
me

a goddess whom i will love
forever

even when she doesn't

love

herself.

i don't have a lot of possessions in my life

i don't have a lot of people in my life

i would lose everything possible

if it meant i would have you.

it's been a long day my love

i sit next to you, picking at my thumbs to keep myself awake

you ask if I want to take a nap

"no," i proclaim

"i like being tired with you."

"i want you in all lifetimes" you said.

"this isn't our first lifetime together" i
assured.

my love, my dear.

i haven't known you long.

we've been through only a couple seasons.

and you give me butterflies.

my love, my dear.

i haven't known you long.

if this phase were to ever pass,

will i still

give you

butterflies?

i can't imagine life without you.

i can't imagine how i would go on with life without you by my side.

i can't imagine how i can just move on.

i can't.

you are my life.

our souls are
tied together
everywhere i go,
i feel you
i feel the love we felt
in our previous lifetime.
i can't wait to
find you
in the
next.

everyone is made up of a little stardust.
many of which came from the same
galaxy.
not us, though.

we came from the same star.

can we be buried together?
can our bodies decompose next to each
other?
can we find each other in the afterlife?
can we scare some kids when we're
ghosts?
can we find our lost pets in heaven?
can we thank god for each other?
can we be buried together holding hands?
can we?

my heart could not stop beating.
i was so nervous.
we sat on a bench.
not saying a word to each other.
we both liked each other.
but too nervous to make a move.
i looked at you, but you didn't look at me.
i wondered what i could do.
i put my arm around you.
you laid on me.
that felt good.
this is good.

i have introduced to you
a love you didn't know was possible,
and now i took your hand
within my heart
and convinced you it is real.

i wish my mind was more developed.
i wish i was able to put all my thoughts
about you into paper.
i wish i paid attention in english class
more.
i wouldn't use words like "love" and
"addicition".
i would spell addiction right.
i would write your name down in my
notebook obsessively.
like it's my trophy.
like you love me.
i wish i was able to put all my thoughts
about you into paper.
because if i could
you would finally believe how much i
love you.

prescribe me your medicine.
be my doctor.
heal me.
talk to me about my body.
tell me what i need to learn.
give me pointers. overstep-
maybe not.

when i'm broken, heal me.

from the moment i met you,
i would die for you.
the singular moment i met you,
the neurons firing in my brain
recognizing a new sight.
the reflections of light
following my cornea
into my optic nerve.
the pictures in my brain
forming of your face.
the thoughts of our future
before i even knew your name.
i, undoubtably,
would die for you.

close your tender eyes.
think of me as you sleep
and whisper into my ear
the sweet nothings of your dreams.
make me so hot that
i am inclined to move away
but choose not to.
when i stay awake
and look at the peaceful drifting of your face
into a realm that i wish i joined.
when i wake up to your hair
brushed across my face
and i move it out my mouth.
when you look at me.
smile.
and crawl out of bed.
but not before you kiss me.
you never forget that part.

i breathe for you.
those moments in between breaths.
that "reset".
i breathe for you.

i hear for you.
that gap between hearing and
understanding.
that "delay".
i hear for you.

i live for you.
that time in between birth and death.
that "journey".
it's for you.
you're the destination.

"you know, i really do like spending time
with you"
"why?"
"i'd much rather sit here in silence with you
than myself"

i was never taught to love.
i never had a good role model to copy what
love should really be.
i felt lost.

then, i met you.
you made loving easy.
i felt like i didn't need to be taught anything.
i felt like i didn't need to prove anything.
you love me, for me.
and i love you, for you.

- i didn't need to be taught

i am helios and you are my moon.
i radiate the earth below me and you help
me in such.
when i can't take the workload,
you help me.
people are more curious about you, though.
everyone is interested in you.
what about me?
im so high and mighty.

i am helios and you are my moon.
i have learned to be a fly on your wall.
i have learned not to care.
although i am the jealous type.

i am helios and you are my moon.
and we are on the same team.
this isn't meant to be a competition.
and i am sorry i turned it into one.
we shine together.
separately, but together.

.

you're so lovely.
watching you eat your oatmeal on my bed
and spilling a little on my blanket.
you panic and clean like i would ever yell.
i never would.
you smile at me, nervously, waiting for a
reaction.
"i love you"
this is our blanket, and it is lovely.

since the day we met i run my fingers over
your body.
"i love you", i spell.
it's soft, my touch.
it's meant for me.

i ask you one day if you know what i write.
"i love you too", you spell.
you knew all along, didn't you.
it's soft, your touch.
it's meant for me.

you play dress up with me.
while i stare at my body in the mirror,
cowering at my own sight.
scared of what you may think.
all you worry about is how this shirt will
match my pants.
how this ring may get caught on my fabric.

essay one

i wonder if i have done anything wrong. i
wonder what you think of me from your
point of view. it stresses me out, knowing
how much i truly love you. all my friends
know about you, they know how much i talk
about you. fuck, i spend most of my time
with you.

but, do i mess up?

i like to think that i don't, you know? i'd
like to think that i've been perfect to you but
we both know that is not the case. truly, im
sorry if i haven't. life has no meaning if
you're not in it. you give the meaning to my
actions every single day and night. you are
responsible for my wake. it is hard to think
that i wrong you, if that is even the case. i
just want you to know that it is not personal.
i want you to realize that everything
negative i do is the result of a fucking
mistake in my head, and that's it. i don't go
out of my way to do wrong. i promise.

you know i love you, and you know i always
will. when i look at you as you walk besides

me, and you hold my arm within yours, i
don't think of the mistakes that i've made
towards you.

i hope, when you look at me as you hold my
arm within yours, that you don't think of it
too.

i am so enthralled by you.
i don't notice the coldness in my heart that
once was.
i don't notice the scorching heat of your soul
melting the ice within mine.
i don't notice the change you have instilled
within me.
i am so enthralled by you, i don't notice the
help you provide.

you've been so great to me.
yes, you.
im not easy to deal with,
and by all means
you are the one who
should be saying this.
im sorry it's not always fun.
but to me,
it's worth it.

i wonder, daily.
simply, wonderfully.
i think, always.
of our future.
simply, beautifully.
i wish, truthfully.
of a home built for two.
a home, for me and you.

look me in my eyes
and tell me im worth it.
don't give up on me.

you're my family now, right?
no, not the type of family that screams at
each other.
not the type of family that drinks too much
on holidays together.
and ends up in fights.
not the family that is only "family" when it
benefits.
not that type of family.

you're my family now, right?
the type of family that goes out for ice
cream on mondays.
and tuesdays.
theres no limit to when they go out for ice
cream.
theres no limit to the love they give.
nothing in return.
no benefits
youre my family now,
and we are getting ice cream.

i had a dream you liked someone else.
silly, i know.
but don't blame my mind for it.

i told you about it.
you laughed, slightly.
"there'll never be another you", you
promised.

- *"don't worry"*

the beauty of our solar system.
unlike anything imaginable.
so close, yet so incomprehensible.
pluto, not a part of it.

why must pluto not be involved.
why must pluto be left out.
he tried his best, he did what he was meant
to do.
not a single orbit was made before pluto was
banished from our system.

not a single chance was given to him.
he couldn't prove himself.

don't let me be pluto.
let me prove myself.
let me be a part of the beauty that is your
solar system.

you have the innate ability to make
anywhere i go, home.

i love doing nothing with you.
sitting back,
reveling in silence.
dancing to nothing.
offkey singing.
wondering when i can do nothing with you
next.

"please, never leave."
i say.
as you look me in my eyes
with the sweetest look.
eyes that will never leave.

your name plagues my notebook.
has ravaged my mind.
taken over my psyche
and trampled over my senses.
you have infected me with your love.
your glory.
i idolize you.

whenever i happen to be alone,

people ask me where you are.

running around like a lost puppy,
i found you.
you took care of me,
and didn't ask any questions.
it's like you were born for this.
it's like
we were born for this.

you saved me.
i saved myself for you.
life is so much brighter with you in it.
so, as you saved me.
please, save yourself.

you
oh, you
you just treat me so good.
im not used to it
i never fathomed
someone like you
love like yours
could ever exist.

you took up my hobbies
you know i like to write,
so write you did.
i like questionable music
and you send me
my favorite artist.
love,
your love,
accepts me.

come on,
come under my blankets
i know your scared
and anxious
you live a stressful life.
but it's okay
im here
and it's quiet.
we can talk about it
if you want.
you don't have to
you know i like to be in silence with you.

you're my best friend
nothing in life will ever
drag me away
from you.

i used to close my eyes
while driving.
step on the gas
and see how long i'd last.
usually i was a coward
and opened my eyes
after a few seconds.
i didn't want to die,
no,
i just didn't care.

when i met you
and you introduced yourself to me
knowing damn well
you knew my name
and i knew yours,
everything changed.

when i searched
up and down
that house party
for some water
because you were thirsty

a person i only knew
for 20 minutes
and a soul
i knew for a lifetime-

-i never closed my eyes driving again
i had bouts
of wanting to
but never did i put myself through that
again.

you opened my eyes
and straightened my wheel
put me in park
and talked to me.

you are why i am here.
you

you,

are the love of my life.

the symphony
of your voice
is one im enamored by.

the melody
of your laugh
is addictive.

the composition
the notes
of your soul
of your smile
let me read you,
let me study you

let me listen to your music
the music of me and you
helios and his moon
the orchestra of us
the lyrics of our life
orbiting
being explored
no one knows the music
of our love
like we do.
you are my moon after
all,
and i am your sun.
our music will be heard
forever.

never
have i ever thought
i would find anyone
who supports me
as much as
you do.

let me cook for you
pasta
the way you like it
but no pepper
you don't like pepper
slightly al dente
i love remembering things about you.

let me
touch your body
worship it
protect it
love it
with no fail.

no amount of distance
mentally,
physically,
emotionally,
will ever make me tired
of you.
i will love you
forever
and this love will never
fade.
we will go through life
together.
and enjoy
what lovely memories
we have yet
to make.

meant to be
me and you
full house in our future
kids running around
positive parenting
one neither of us had.
cats
or dogs
we haven't had that conversation
yet.
maybe even a lizard
with a funny name.
anything life throws at us
as long as i have you
it's a life worth living.

everyday
i live out
the dreams i have
of you

you are the
only person
who has convinced me
happiness
will forever
be an understatement.

take my hand
within yours and protect me
love me
unconditionally
and introduce me to
your family.
we are family now
after all,
im drawn
to your orbit.

for the last time,
i'll never leave you.
ever.
never once has it
been an option.
i vow
to protect you
from the monsters
under your bed.
i will love you
until the end of time
and beyond that,
whatever it may be.

you have given me
the happiest moments
of my life,
and i will
forever
be indebted to you.

there is no miracle
other than me and you.
helios and his moon
orbit your world
and i will shine my light
on it.
the remnants of our past
watered
by the miracle
of our future.

his moon

the following poems are of everything
negative that can happen within a
relationship. it may be about jealousy,
cheating, abuse, death, and the likes. some
poems stretch the same idea amongst
multiple pages, while others are only a few
words. regardless, love can always feel.
whatever can happen, will happen. it is up to
the people within the relationship to stop it
from happening. it is up to helios and his
moon to stay a team.

many poems within this section cover
sensitive topics.

if i were to die,
my soul would grieve for you.
i would haunt you, terrify you,
and make my presence known.
i will never stop being around you.

if i were to die,
my soul would grieve for you.
i would be at my own funeral,
watching you cry over me.
i will never stop watching you.

if you were to move on,
find love,
and forget me,

i would die once more.

i will grieve.

i found my place on these clouds.
looking down towards society.
this can't be heaven.
i don't see you.
where are you?
i am scared.
please.

where
are you?

my days came to an end.
i fell asleep
and fell into a desolate void.
it's pitch black.
i can't see anything.

i see a hand reach out for me.
it is you.

we are back in our home.
on our couch.
with the tv playing
and everything is okay.

let us be astronauts
floating in the dark abyss above
getting caught in an atmosphere
unable to leave.

brought into a planet
the panicked beeping of our ship
the panicked breathing of our bodies.

we won't make it back home today.
we may never make it back.
but I have you.
i close my eyes for the last time.
thank you.

if you had the chance to go back to your
childhood
carefree
resilient
and comfortable,
but no one would join you
would you take that chance?
would you leave me?

i cuddle this stuffed animal to sleep every
night.
it watches me cry.
it watches me laugh.
i don't want to spray your perfume on this
stuffed animal.
i don't want to yell at it.
please stay.

diary #1

     i am so afraid to lose her oh my god i love her so fucking much. we held hands today in the parking lot and listened to queen and it was beautiful. i saw a tear flow down her face and i don't know what i did wrong but i need her in my life and oh my god i am about to cry. did i do anything wrong. i want her in my life so fucking bad i want her to be mine but i don't think she wants to. i love her so much.

                              nicholas

we were never meant to work.

we were doomed from the

start.

why do people celebrate sunsets?
as they are the start of the night,
the end of all that is day.
the beauty of the journey is blinding,
outshined by the beauty of the end.

i know you've forgotten about me.
admit it, you have.
i don't think you'd even recognize me.
im grown now.
more mature.
i finally learned that song you always liked.
and,
for the last time,
you forgot about me.

why
do you consistently
betray me
go behind my back
and stab me with your
brutal words
and
broken promises
and how do you
manage to
keep pulling me in?

as i sit on this bench
someone looks just like you
walking by
walks the same, too.
i can't help but think of
when you
had me tie your shoes
and hold your keys.
when you watched me play the piano
and couldn't help but smile
and wonder what i'll play at our wedding.
but they walked past now
and they're just a person

- and you're just a memory

what if you found someone better
better looking, maybe
more money
they have those green eyes you always
wanted
i'd choose them, too

but why not me?

brown eyes are golden under the sun.

pov I

it's been 1 month and i've moved on
they took so much out of me in this
relationship
and i'm just glad it's over.
i can have fun now
do what i always wanted
i can play the piano in peace now.

it's been 4 months and i am sad.
not depressed
not numb
sad.
i feel lonely
let me go out again.
let me play the piano and get my mind off
them.

it's been 1 year and i miss them.
their brown hair
curly
soft.
eyes as bright as the sun.
mind as clear as day.
every key on this piano is another memory
of them.

pov II

it's been 1 month and i'm a wreck.
every day and night i go to bed and wake up
crying
and it won't stop no matter how hard i try.
i can't bear to look at a piano

it's been 4 months and i'm getting there.
one step at a time
deep breath
in
out.

it's been a year and i miss them.
i hope they're doing well.
i took up piano lessons and they'd be proud
of me.
i met someone.
i am clouded by memories.
every key on this piano feels familiar.
as if someone
somewhere
is also playing the same keys.

you planted flowers on my grave and i
watched every second of it
you didn't move on
you loved me too much
it's unfair you couldn't come along

i watched as you walked into your bedroom
and pulled out pills
what are you doing

you went to sleep
wake up

what are you doing

i felt at home for once
i watched your soul come for me
tried to reach me
but you never could

you loved me too much.
it's unfair you couldn't come along.

come back
it was just an argument
and i didn't mean what i said
come on you know i love you
there there
good
you need to learn to trust me you know
you need to put in more effort.

why did you have to go
and leave me here
alone
i am helios and you were my moon
we were supposed to be a team
teams don't split up
it was supposed to be me and you
who is supposed to reflect my light now

i don't know where you are
and im scared
and i want you back
please
come back

- denial

i gave you my word
i promised
that you were the only one
that you would be my number one pick
forever
you were my soulmate
you couldn't even respect that
you treated me like a caged animal
giving affection only when i too weak to
fight back
cornered
scared
you embarrassed me
and i loved you.

i am tired of you
you did nothing wrong
surely, you didn't
in fact you were great
you did everything right
yet
i am tired of you

i am helios and you are my moon
and i don't want you anymore
you take the attention away from me
and i have no use for you.
we were on the same team
and we did well
but people are enamored by you
and i am left in your darkness.
let me spread my wings moon
let me leave
i have no use for you.
i am helios and you are my moon
and we should shine separately.

i loved you deeply.
once.
we were perfect together.
and i couldn't imagine what life would be
without you.
once.
now you don't even look at me in the halls.
you walk faster.
pretend i never existed.
like i once did.

you invited me to your room
for the first time
and i glanced around eagerly
the room i saw in so many photos.
i met your family
for the first time
and they already knew
so much about me
and i knew so much
about them.
we never kissed, me and you.
we never even held hands.
but losing you
was the greatest loss
the greatest mistake.

and i loved you with all my heart.
so deeply
and you made a mistake.
so unforgivable.
took advantage of me
my temple
and left me to crumble.
you are inconceivably evil.

please, let me move on.
stop coming back into my life
expecting me to take you back
you are prolonging my grief
you are torturing me
leave me alone
for good.

do you still wear my clothes to sleep
do they still smell like me
do you think of my touch
do you remember
how many freckles i have
or what my eyes look like?

the beautiful shade of your eyes
one that i will never forget

- no matter how hard i try

i loved when you came over
watched shows with me
played with my fingers
and run them on your skin.
i loved when you played
with my stuffed animals
gave them your own names
and called them our children.
and i loved being yours
for the infinitely little time we had together
i loved it

i wish you did
too

our friendly competitions
who can race down the hall faster
who can do the most pushups
who loves each other more.

"i love you"
"i love you more"

no,

i love you more.

you have been the only person
in my world
to show me soulmates
aren't always meant
to be.

my brain cannot fathom
consistently
being the second choice
being second to everything in your life
you promised me love
so many times
and took it back each time
and took parts of me with you

you're gone
forever
all i have are your memories in my head
your smell on my sweater
your letters to me
your ghost on my hand.

at least here,
in my mind,
my sweater,
my drawer,
and my hand,

we're happy
and you're here
with me.

im happy it's over
and you've moved on
while i haven't.
we were never meant to happen
but yet we did

we tried
and it didn't work
as much as i tried
and as much as you didn't.

im so sorry
to treat you the way i did
to yell at you
and call you the words
that should never be said
by anyone
in love with someone.
you didn't deserve it
you didn't deserve me.

leave me.
walk away from me
and never keep in touch
be my stranger
you are disgusting
and i never want to see you again.
leave me.

i wanted to grow with you
me and you, together
and grow old.
have a welcome mat
in front of our door
with a bunch of cats
and a stone fireplace.
two
maybe three kids
so they can make decisions for themselves
no ties
someone would be a tiebreaker.
with a nice piano
not too expensive
but one that would last us
until we were old.
a beautiful yard
with an avocado tree
and maybe a lemon tree
so we don't always
need to go to the store
but i wouldn't have
minded that
either,
i loved walking with you.
we would've had a small wedding
not small
sorry-

-i know you always corrected me on that
but not big either
medium sized
in the woods
or nature
because you always looked beautiful in
green.
honeymoon in italy
celebrating
a life we would never have
with what we couldn't afford.
hobbies to pick up together
tennis
running
writing
our list went on.
you always insisted on
decorating our house
and while i reluctantly agreed
i agreed nonetheless.
i wanted to grow with you
me and you, together
and grow old.

- was that all for nothing?

the hands
that touched my body
for the first time-
i forgot what they feel like

i loved the smell
of my skin
after we hung out.
the smile on
my face
when you told me you
loved me.
but
at some point
how much love
can you really take?

you used to
dress me up
you told me to change
my hair
and my shoes
you really didn't
like my shoes
you gave me rings
to wear
and switched out
my glasses
for cuter ones.
did you treat me
so well
or did you mold me
into the person
you always wanted?

i cannot fathom
you ever cheating on me.
you have done nothing
nothing
to prove to me that you would,
yet,
jealous i am.
you tell me
i will always be the
only one
so why do i still
feel this way?

the endless void
that is the afterlife
is one i fall into
away from the vision
that i once had.
you're old
wrinkly
that cute shirt i always
liked
and you're using
all your strength to stand.
the vision is fading
that i once had
and soon
i will just
be a memory
to you.

i called your name out
and i never heard back
you ran away from me
when i needed you most
i just wanted love
i was getting better.

our relationship was 50/50.
a phrase heard a lot,
but deadly
how false it is.
should never be 50/50.
why put half effort
in something
that lasts you
until infinity?

you used to
always sing this song
incorrectly
you never knew the lyrics
and i never bothered to
correct you,
you just seemed so happy to
be with me.
i have a feeling you
knew it,
too.
you knew the lyrics
all along
but were too afraid
to admit it.
you probably just
made a mistake the first
time you sang to me,
and went with it.
dwelling on your mistakes
never correcting it
thinking it was cute.
it was never about lyrics
or a song
and we were never
about music.

you hindered our growth
dramatically
i was never afraid to
grow alongside you,
i was afraid
of your reaction
to growing.

forever
never
existed
for
us

we used to
sit back
and have movie marathons
and never knew
what the movies were about
because we'd
stare at each other
the entire time.
and figured out
to ditch the popcorn
because it made
your tongue
taste weird when
we kissed.
now
i sit here
like a fool
knowing exactly
what these movies
are about.

will you ever make
time for me?
you told me you would
but
you've left me in
your darkness
wondering
where the time has gone.

the constant cycle
of being left
for being boring
or losing feelings
instantly
is draining.
it's why
i constantly ask you

- do you still like me?

walk out that door
and don't come back
never look back at the
holes you have made
in the walls
or the dishes
you've thrown
at me.

walk out my life
and never look back
at what you have caused
my future
loves.

stop drinking
and telling me you love me
for the sole reason
that you won't remember it
in the morning.

i never would've chosen you.
you kept pulling me in
and gave me no choice
but to choose you.
you gave me a false
sense of
security.
a false sense of love.
and made me
forget
who i really am.

you never loved me
for who i really was.
you always tried
changing me
and convinced me
i am the worst
person alive.
yelling the worst things
someone can yell.
all because
in your eyes
i was the bad one.

driving back that night
you made me take your
friends
because they couldn't
take themselves.
doing you a favor
that night
after you told me
you never really loved me.
i would've crashed that car
if i was alone
but they didn't deserve that

- and neither did i

what will
our pets think
now that you're
gone?

through the end
of time itself-

-i feel like
i'll love you.
as much i don't
want to
nor feel like
you deserve it.
-

-i just believe
we are soulmates.
and meant to be
even if we don't
think we are.
as much as i love you-

-and care for you
unlike anyone you've met
i don't feel-

-like you'll ever
love me back
or care for me
unless i asked.

feel it

within this section, the work provided will
help simulate a relationship. from the
beginning to inevitable end, pieces of work
will help describe, vaguely and specifically,
how relationships work. this may include
trust, fear of the unknown, and puppy love.
however, this is not all.
enjoy helios finding his moon.

the following poems may contain
troublesome topics.

checking me in
to an event
a lovely girl
never got her name
but radiated energy
unlike no other.

being teased by
friends when i asked them
if i thought
they were into me.
all i wanted to know
was if i found
something real.

she asked around, too
her coworkers
if they thought i was into
her.
again,
they teased her
relentlessly.

never saw her again,
gone with the wind
i felt her
gravitational pull
from around.
i am her sun
and she doesn't yet know
that she is my moon.

the radiance
of her smile
changed my life from
the moment i saw her.
i knew
somehow
she would be
the one.

i once
used to sit on this
bench
wondering where
my life would take me
but now
as this person walks by
i realized
they walk just like you
and you're not just
a memory

- you're my future

and once
she found my smile
at that party
she knew
it was her chance
to talk to me
for i was
too scared.

that halloween party
i painted my face to hide
my identity from people
to hide my eyebags
to hide the fact that i cried the hour before
to hide the fact i was young
to see who would approach me
to see who wouldn't
i painted my face to hide my identity from
people
but you saw past that
you chose me out of everyone in that crowd
and never gave up
you never gave up on me.

you figured my heart out
a feat i never knew
could be accomplished
a girl
who assured me
we've been together
in another life.

i am helios
and i want you to
be my moon
i want to supply
the world
you are orbiting
and i want
to be
a team.

i promise i'm trying
thank you for believing
in me
but please
believe in me some more
give me time
to heal
and accept
the love
you are so graciously
offering.

let me write
you this book
and keep it with you
at all times
take care of it
and make sure
nothing happens to it
never read the next page
until you feel
as if you are ready
to start a life
with me.

you took care of this book
with all your might
and subconsciously
took care of us.
you may not have been ready
to be with me
but it is okay
im patient.
i waited
and i could've waited
as long as
you wanted.
thank you for reading this
page
and now,
please,
be mine.

the glory
that is you
the healing
that is you.
you have changed
me
and i
forever
will love you for it.

no painting
in any museum
will compare to
the artwork
that i find
when i look into
your eyes.

you are
the embodiment
of perfection
health,
and all that is my soul.
you are my
mirror reflection
my other half
and my reason
to keep going.

its okay
don't be mad
we'll work through this,
okay?
it was one mistake
and i know you
know that.
i trust you
so much
and i want
that same trust
from you.

the sun sets
and i am starting to see
why people
celebrate.
it is not always
about the end,
rather,
the beauty that is the
journey
towards
purple skies.

as helios rises
above the horizon
the moon hides
in the shadows
dancing amongst the cosmos
enamored at the light
helios provides.
this is finally
what it is like
to be a team.

take my hand
and dance with me
in this kitchen.
red wine drunkenness
and lovesick melodies
of our soul
diffuse
through our feet
onto this tile floor.
weird smelling breath
and glossy eyes
will only be remembered
in the morning.
for now,
may the only memories
be of us
dancing
with no care in the world.

i am so glad
that you are mine.
that you trusted me
enough
to change our worlds
and combine them
into one.

from a painted face
in a room full
of strangers
to finding my own future
within your face.

i would love
for our kids
to have your nose
eyes
no,
eye shape
hair type.
they can have my
eye color
lips
and eyebrows.
and we
will be such
a happy family.

it's been a year
and i want to marry you.
you, however
want to wait
and that is completely
okay.
as long
as i have you
i will wait for you
however long
it may be.

a ring
fit for a queen
on your finger.
young,
troublesome,
and madly in love.
never get into fights
besides that nasty one
a few years back.
just two kids
with goals
and ambitions
that love each other.

i am so
proud
of all that you
have accomplished
my love.

"GOOD MORNING MY LOVE"
- 9:29 am

"HEYY"
- 9:54 am

"I MISSED U"
- 9:54 am

"how'd u sleep ?"
-9:55 am

"i slept good i just kept waking up a lot"
- 9:58 am

"wbu?"
- 10:01 am

"yeah same i couldn't really sleep that
much"
- 10:04 am

"i hate that ur not here rn"
- 10:05 am

"ughh me too"
- 10:09 am

"i just wish you could've came to the hotel
w me"
- 10:10 am

                              "me too :("
                              - 10:10 am

              "are u excited for ur interview ?"
                              - 10:12 am

"umm im kinda excited"
"mostly just anxious tho"
- 10:13 am

                    "i understand my love"
                  "everything will be alright"
                   "i have full faith in you"
                          "i love you"
                          - 10:15 am

"i love you too"
- 10:16 am

"ughh ur so good to me"
- 10:17 am

"and ur so good to me :)"
"what are u wearing ?"
- 10:21 am

"uhh just some pj bottoms and a tank top"
- 10:23 am

"no dumbass"
"what are u wearing to ur interview"
- 10:24 am

"LMAOOO"
"that was funny"
"i'll prob just wear my black slacks and a
white cardigan"
- 10:26 am

"LMAO"
"aww ur so cute"
"i know ur gonna do so good"
- 10:30 am

"thank you babe :)"
"what time do you work today?"
- 10:31 am

"12-5:30"
"what time is ur interview again ?"
- 10:32 am

"nice nice"
"its at 11:30"
- 10:34 am

"WTF"
"isn't it like a 20 mik drive??"
"**min"
- 10:34 am

"YES but its okay ill be there on time"
"don't you worry ur pretty lil brain"
- 10:36 am

"okayy whatever you say my love"
- 10:38 am

"are u gonna eat anything before ?"
- 10:40 am

"yes sir im gonna get some brekkie at the
buffet rn"
- 10:41 am

"i'll be quick tho don't worry"
- 10:42 am

"okay just making sure :)"
"u can lag if you want i'll just be here"
- 10:44 am

"OKAY i wont be gone for long i promise"
"SEEYA SOON ILY"
- 10:45 am

"OKAY ILYM"
- 10:45 am

"HEYY"
"guess whos back"
- 11:07 am

> "HEY i missed u"
> "you really should go get ready"
> "its getting pretty late"
> - 11:07 am

"don't stress me out"
"imma get ready rn"
- 11:08 am

> "okay ur right my bad"
> "lmk when ur on ur way :)"
> -11:08 am

"OKAY i just finished and imma head out
rn"
"i gotta be quick im running a lil late"
- 11:15 am

> "OKAY BE SAFEE"
> - 11:15 am

"BYE I LOVE U SO MUCH"
- 11:15 am

"SORRY for the lag"
"i was playing the piano then showered"
"but ur prob in ur interview rn"
"UR DOING GREAT"
- 11:41 am

"imma be at work and can't text until my
break"
"ILL SEE U LATERRR"
- 11:47 am

"HEY im on my break"
"wya"
- 3:20 pm

"did u do good?"
- 3:27 pm

"ur probably napping or something so just
text me whenever"
- 3:30 pm

"HEY im back"
-5:34 pm

"wya?"
- 5:38 pm

"why is ur location off"
- 5:47 pm

"are u sleeping?"
-6:01 pm

"ur worrying me"
-6:10 pm

"why aren't u picking up ur phone"
-6:39 pm

"ur really scaring me baby"
-6:51 pm

"this cant be fucking happening"
-8:12 pm

"im so sorry i couldn't say bye to you please
just respond to me i love you so much
please this cant be happening please why
did they say you got in a car accident"
- 8:14 pm

"please pick up please they are lying please i
love you so much you don't deserve this"
- 8:15 pm

"ur family keeps calling me but i don't want
to pick up"
"why do they keep texting me please this
isn't real"
- 8:16 pm

"i just talked to the police they came to our
door"
- 10:39 pm

"you were supposed to be home today"
- 10:45 pm

"its been a month my love. i am a fucking wreck. ive lost 20 pounds because i haven't eaten. the cats don't know where you are"
- 1:17 am

"i love you so much i will never love again please come back"
- 1:19 am

"goodnight my love"
- 2:11 am

"its been 3 months baby. our cat died. im so
sorry. i haven't brought myself to leave and
get him food. i guess he ran out."
- 5:07 pm

"please forgive me i didn't mean for him to
die"
"this is all my fault"
- 5:09 pm

"you were the brightest smile ive ever seen"
"are*"
- 5:10 pm

"its been 3 months wife. im starting to gain
my weight back but i need to go to therapy
or i may not last much longer."
- 4:45 pm

"We're sorry, the number you have tried to
reach is no longer in service. If you feel this
is an issue, please contact your provider.
Thank you."
- 4:45 pm

"FUCK YOU"
- 4:46 pm

"We're sorry, the number you have tried to
reach is no longer in service. If you feel this
is an issue, please contact your provider.
Thank you."
- 4:46 pm

"its been a year baby. ive been trying not to
text so i don't get that damn robot response.
let me update you. i got a new cat! im
writing that poetry book i always told you
about. thinking of naming it helios with his
moon, what do you think? i met someone.
please don't be upset, theyre good. they
know all about you, i cant stop talking about
you. they have been taking me to therapy
and even the therapist agrees i shouldn't
dwell on the past. i really wish we had a life
together, i really do. its funny, sometimes i
sit on this bench and this girl walks by and
all i think about is holding your keys, even
tying ur shoes. just the small things, yk? im
starting to forget what you smelled like. and,
as much as i want to forget, i cannot get
your eyes out of my head. i also moved
apartments, and it almost brought me to
death to give away all the stuff you left here.
no, actually, helios and his moon sounds
better to me. sorry i just feel-
-like we haven't spoken in a while. don't
think ive ever forgotten you. i never will,
you will always be the love of my life. my
soulmate. i grieve every single day for you.
and, now, it's time we both should move on.
i feel your presence watching me. judging

me at times, but its cute. i should get going
now, i need to get ready for my date. i love
you so much, goodbye."
- 6:26 pm

"Sorry man, you have the wrong number."
- 7:01 pm

"i cant fucking take this anymore. its been a year and a half and ever since they gave ur number away i haven't fucking recovered. WHO GAVE UR FUCKING NUMBER AWAY? i broke it off with the girl and let her take the damn cat with her too. i quit my job and im behind on rent. i miss you so much i want to join you. please let me join you. im so tired baby please. i've already sent the letters to my family and friends and warned everyone. no one wanted to stop me. no one seemed to care. i planted these last flowers on your grave. im so tired. i took so many pills and im gonna go to sleep now. i cannot wait to see you my love, you have no idea. ive missed you. see you soon"

- what are you doing

"Woah what the fuck? Are you okay man?
Do you need me to call some help?"

"Dude?"

"Hello?"

biography

nicholas mcdaniel is a creative writer from downey, california. he has written two unpublished poetry books, and they were regarded so highly by peers- that he decided to write *helios and his moon*. his first published work, it tackles the beautiful, yet, intense reality of love. nicholas is an avid piano player, and finds most of his inspiration behind those keys. nicholas thoroughly enjoys writing anything about the human psyche, including themes of love, healing, and grief. he is constantly supported by his family, friends, and loving partner, and dedicates all work to them. without them, of course, he wouldn't be here today.

reach out!

nmcdanielwriting@gmail.com
ig: heirofhelios

Made in United States
Troutdale, OR
09/14/2023

12868037R00108